CROSS~COUNTRY RIDING

WITHOUT THE COURAGE AND
THE TRUST OF HIS HORSE, THE
RIDER IS NOTHING

Lucinda Green

CROSS~COUNTRY RIDING

WITH PHOTOGRAPHS BY
KIT HOUGHTON

PELHAM BOOKS
LONDON

First published in Great Britain by
Pelham Books Ltd
27 Wrights Lane
London W8
1986

British Library Cataloguing in Publication Data
Green, Lucinda
    Cross-country riding.
    1. Cross-country (Horsemanship)
    I. Title
    798.2′3   SF295.6

    ISBN 0-7207-1696-9

Printed and bound in Great Britain
by Butler & Tanner Ltd, Frome and London

To Be Fair and
those special ones
that followed him

Contents

Acknowledgements

To John Burbidge and SR International who have set an example of unbending support and encouragement to David and me through times good and lean.

To all those who over the years have given me the benefit of their experience.

To all those who have been and still are involved in producing the competitions that enable us to take up the challenge that cross-country presents.

To Lord and Lady Hugh Russell, over whose unique Wylye cross-country facilities many of the photographs were taken.

To photographer Kit Houghton and editor Lesley Gowers who are a joy to work with and to whom nothing is ever too much trouble.

Photo credits

All the photographs in this book are by Kit Houghton, except pictures 1–3 on pages 116–17, which were taken by Stuart Newsham.

Preface

This book is a collection of thoughts promoted by my experiences of riding across country over the last few years.

Inevitably I have come to believe in certain methods of tackling different situations, just as I have become convinced of the simple fundamentals to cross-country success. Not everyone will agree with what is said, for after all, there are many ways to catch a fish. This book is simply my interpretation of a wealth of generous advice and a number of years learning from my mistakes.

It is written in tremendous admiration for horses. Most will tolerate being ridden in a variety of different styles and still try their hardest to negotiate a fence.

To them and to those people who have been such great sources of aid and counsel over the years, I offer my deepest thanks. The immense thrills and overall enjoyment throughout my eventing life, I doubt I could have found anywhere else.

The abundance of photographs of me are herein on Publisher's orders, and it is regretted that so many appear to show me doing something right – it certainly does not happen as frequently as this book may have people believe. Furthermore I would like to apologise to the riders whose photographs were taken at an unfortunate moment.

Finally, it should be noted that the contents of this book are specifically concerned with helping people ride across country. Much of what is written therefore does not apply to other forms of jumping.

PART 1

Balance

The foundation of riding, like almost everything around us, rests on one word: balance.

Balance comes to some more naturally than to others, but it is something that can be learned. It may take hours or it may take years of practice, but the more a person rides the better his balance will become. Gradually he will begin to sit deeper into his horse and feel less perched on top. One day, when he finds he can sit to a buck or an awkward jump, then an independent seat is beginning to develop. Any rider who, often subconsciously, still relies on his reins to stay in the saddle, is not yet secure in his seat.

When a child learns to ride he is taught to hold on to the front of the saddle or the mane, or both at once. Just as he struggled and wobbled when he was a baby, until finally he could stand without support, so he will, little by little, learn to find his balance on a pony. Eventually he will discover that he can let go of the mane and the saddle and still feel safe.

The balance needed while riding on the flat and that needed while jumping fences is different. Often people will find themselves capable and secure on the flat, only to be reduced to feeling like a beginner again once they start jumping.

Some find a natural balance when their legs are at full length, others when their knees are tucked under their chin. Hence, some feel happy doing dressage while others prefer riding racehorses. The real horseman, I believe, is capable of balancing himself throughout the spectrum of lengths of leg and is able to do well in any of the different sports to which they apply.

Certainly I am only really happy in cross-country length. Shorter, and I feel I will fall off; longer, and I do not feel I have so much control of the horse's or my own balance.

A number of people do ride too long across country, possibly under the false impression that they can use their legs more. It is very difficult to balance a horse across country with long stirrups, and until he is in balance, it will not be easy for him to perform well.

Success in learning to walk, skate, ski, play ball games, live a happy life, or ride, is apparent once the pupil has finally found the required balance in whatever aspect he is attempting. How good he becomes at his pursuit thereafter, depends largely on the amount of work he is able to put into practising.

Indeed there are always some people with more natural ability than others. Those who are naturally talented do not necessarily succeed because very often they never learn to work at it; things come too easily to them.

In 1974, multiple show-jumping Olympic gold medallist, Hans Winkler, watched me ride for a while, before giving me a lesson. After a prolonged silence, eventually he exclaimed, 'What sort of a horse is this Be Fair then – if he can win Badminton in spite of you?'

Later he was responsible for giving me the trickle of hope which, during the years that followed, has seen me through many low ebbs. 'Riding is an art that *can* be taught – you don't have to be born with it.' He told me that he had not been born with it and he assured me that I had not either.

Once the independence of seat from hands has been achieved, it is a wonderful feeling. It reminds me of the moment when my bicycle first stayed in a straight line and did not turn into a frenzied snake when I let go of the handlebars. Riding a bike without hands is the nearest description I can find to equate with the feeling of being able to stay on a horse without the security of the reins.

It is this independence of seat from hands which forms the foundation of confidence for the horse across country.

A horse relies on the freedom of his head and neck to balance himself. If he is studied as he gallops loose in the field, twisting, turning and cavorting, the amount he moves his head and neck and the radius through which they can travel are remarkable. Unless he slips, an unmounted horse will very rarely fall over, whatever he is doing, because he has no impediment to his balance.

To be a good cross-country rider it is imperative to be able to give the horse freedom of his head and neck at any moment he should need it. This will create in the horse a base of trust in his rider, but it can only be achieved if the rider is entirely secure and balanced in his own seat.

Apart from restricting this freedom, the worst mistake a rider can make across country is to be in front of the horse's movement. Being in such a position makes it very difficult for the rider to feel what the horse is about to do and to be able to take any corrective

measures that may become necessary to help prevent the horse running out, stopping or even falling. It is also a great deal more difficult not to fall off when the horse makes a bad mistake if the rider is in front of the movement.

The ideal is a rider in the centre of balance with his horse. To err on the side of being left behind is infinitely preferable to being in front. However, it is of the utmost importance that the horse does not have his freedom interrupted by a pull back on the reins if the rider is left behind.

Generally the most effective and secure

place to be when riding into a cross-country fence, jumping it and landing over it, is a fraction behind the centre of balance.

Until some riders see videos or photos of themselves, they often will not believe that they are 'in front' of the horse. Riders are sometimes told to sit up straighter as they approach a difficult fence, and whilst they are sure they are doing just that, they often only manage to straighten their crouch horizontally, instead of vertically.

Initially we are taught the forward seat on the approach to a jump and over

ABOVE LEFT: *The rider is behind the movement but is offering the horse complete freedom of his head and neck.*

ABOVE RIGHT: *Another example of a rider being behind the movement and slipping the reins to give the horse his freedom.*

ABOVE LEFT: *A rider in front of the movement.*

ABOVE RIGHT: *The most sensitive part of the average horse is his mouth. It is important, however strong a horse is, not to hold on to his mouth over a fence.*

it. It is necessary to learn in this way, or the rider would be left behind and probably pull on the horse's mouth over each jump. Very soon the horse would refuse to jump any more because of such discomfort.

As the rider develops better balance and independence he can become more a part of the horse and slowly begin to influence *how* they approach each obstacle.

My 13.2 hh New Forest pony, Jupiter, taught me forcibly those two most important lessons at the age of nine. If I was not constantly 'in behind him', he would refuse. If I pulled his mouth over a fence he would stop at the next one.

At that early age he also taught me another important lesson: the timing of using my whip. Often he did not quite hear what my weak, skinny legs were trying to tell him and I *had* to find an extra aid. Too many people, especially when they are beginning, are over-wary of using a whip. 'Spare the rod and spoil the child' applies absolutely to horses too. If you are prepared to use the whip, horses rarely seem to need it. Infrequently it needs to be used as a punishment but more often as an extra aid, or as an encouragement, during a moment of doubt in the horse or indeed the rider.

Surprisingly few people are truly aware of the importance of not holding on to a horse's mouth over a fence. When it is analysed, the importance becomes clearer.

The most sensitive part of the average horse is his mouth, into this is put a bit, attached to which are some reins. The rider holds the reins with varying degrees of strength and sometimes can swing his whole weight on them if he loses balance.

The horse's balancing-pole is his head and neck; he needs to be able to do with that whatever is necessary to balance himself and perform. If he feels a pull on his mouth over each fence, he is unlikely to stretch out his neck towards that pull, therefore he will very quickly learn to compensate by jumping in a restricted fashion. Some horses reach great heights having adjusted thus, but most never realise their full potential or place their entire trust in their rider. Some riders allow their horse freedom on take-off and in mid-air over the jump. Then maybe they start thinking subconsciously about the ground coming up towards them and never give the horse the extra rein that he needs to stretch out his neck on the descent. Without the freedom in the last third of the jump, the horse will bring up his head too quickly and hollow. He will find it difficult to jump properly and will soon start to lose confidence.

From reading this, many may feel that

Without his freedom in the last third of the jump, the horse will bring up his head too quickly and hollow.

it is probably wisest to drop the reins altogether just before take-off and then there can be no danger of catching the horse in the mouth. Although some high-class show-jumping riders do exactly this, it is not desirable across country. A horse can learn very quickly to duck out when suddenly he feels the contact dropped. Most horses seem to like an even contact and feel lost and insecure when it disappears at the moment they are preparing to take off.

Finally riders, however well practised, seldom find themselves perfectly and centrally balanced over a fence. It is useful therefore for the rider to remember one thing when feeling out of balance over a fence: to open the fingers. Wherever the rider is, and however unbalanced he has become, the horse will most probably manage, provided his rider has remembered to open his fingers and let the reins slip through to give the horse his full freedom.

The Horse

No matter how good the rider, no one can make a horse do anything he does not want to. The training of any horse needs to be carried out with this firmly borne in mind.

When the jumping training of a horse begins, he should never be asked to jump anything that he could not negotiate out of a standstill. If a horse learns to refuse and has to be turned away from a fence at a very early stage in his training, the habit will be easily formed.

Usually the horse picks up confidence quite quickly while trotting over small jumps and often becomes casual or flippant about them. If so, then it is time to approach fences that are a little bigger, but still out of trot. Some horses need to mingle this with cantering over a few as well; others, maybe those with hotter temperaments, will be better jumping only out of trot in the early stages.

All the way through his career, a horse will tell his rider, if the latter listens, when he is ready to move on up the ladder. Similarly when he starts competing, he will indicate when he is ready to move from Novice standard to Intermediate and ultimately on to Advanced.

Whilst a horse is still backing off, spooking at his fences and generally feeling unsure, then he is not ready to move on to greater things. Some spook purely out of naughtiness and boredom; and such animals may need to be presented with more of a challenge to channel their active minds. The rider can soon tell whether his horse is lacking in confidence or is in fact over-confident.

It is always best to err on the side of taking a horse too slowly through the stages, rather than too quickly. Many more horses have been ruined through not spending long enough thoroughly learning the elementary lessons, than they have been through spending too long at them.

I find the longest part of training horses is usually from their beginning through to the end of Novice event standard. Thereafter, they often graduate more quickly because they are then building on firm foundations.

Throughout his training, the objective the horse is being encouraged to achieve is something of a paradox: *He is being asked to think for himself, but at the same time he must listen to his rider and learn obedience.*

Hunting is a wonderful education ground for young horses, unless their temperament is very hot. They learn self-preservation and sure-footedness, but it can also be tough on them. For this reason I would not hunt a four-year-old and only a five-year-old lightly.

It is wise to remember that a horse rarely comes to full maturity before seven years old. Many do not mature until they are nine or ten.

If a five- or six-year-old is asked to do hard work such as full-scale three-day events or regular fast team 'chases it may well foreshorten the span of his sound and working life.

It takes several years of bringing a horse to full fitness before he becomes as fit as he can be. It is interesting that the greatest test of a cross-country horse, Badminton, has been won predominantly by mature horses whose ages have reached double figures.

Most horses thoroughly enjoy jumping once they have found their confidence. Occasionally I meet one who does not like it and normally there is a reason for this. Either he has been frightened when jumping earlier, or he has some pain somewhere when he jumps. It has to be accepted that there are, however, some horses who do not obtain a thrill from it and such individuals are best left alone.

If the rider loves to go across country, in time he will inspire that joy into most horses. There is no point, and it is definitely no fun, going over solid fences across awkward country on a horse who does not enjoy it. Sooner or later the rider knows it will end in tears. It is best to accept defeat before that point is reached.

Type of Horse

There are few rules about what makes a good cross-country horse. All kinds appear out hunting, at hunter trials, team 'chases and events. If the ambition of the rider is to scale the heights and to win, then it is necessary for the horse to possess a generous amount of 'blood'. A heavy, lesser quality horse will find it very difficult to maintain the required speeds for long enough.

Buying a potential cross-country horse is a blindman's choice. The most promising youngster can turn out not to have quite enough courage or athleticism when he is ultimately tested. Whereas, the most ordinary or nervous horse can develop into the best. The buyer has to

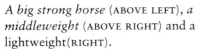
A big strong horse (ABOVE LEFT), *a
middleweight* (ABOVE RIGHT) and a
lightweight(RIGHT).

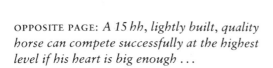
OPPOSITE PAGE: *A 15 hh, lightly built, quality
horse can compete successfully at the highest
level if his heart is big enough …*

... as can a 17.2 hh quality horse.

rely on a gut feeling and reasonable certainty that the horse's conformation, particularly his limbs, are built well enough to withstand the inevitable strains that will be placed on them.

Cross-country is a tough game for a horse that is not made right. It discovers the flaws in a horse's mechanics. If he is in proportion and put together correctly, he will not find any difficulty withstanding the rigours.

A heavier horse with less quality will find it difficult to make winning times in big events, but will quite often be a safe conveyance.

Bitting

Controlling a horse who has found his confidence and discovered the joys of cross-country can cause problems.

Many horses pull for reasons other than keenness, though. Often it emanates either from discomfort or a lack of confidence in themselves or their riders. There may be a problem with the teeth, or perhaps the inside of the mouth is torn and painful. Maybe a bar of the mouth has even been broken at some time, or possibly the horse is wrong in

his back. Crossing his jaw or putting his tongue over a bit slung too low in his mouth, also causes pulling.

Frequently a horse will pull if the rider pulls. Some riders make almost any horse strong. Some horses require such a fine degree of contact that if the rider is not aware of it, he will hold on too hard and send the horse crazy.

When Regal Realm first came to me in 1980, he was extremely strong; he had been ridden in a gag. He ewed his neck,

BELOW LEFT: A rubber gag with flash noseband. This is an experienced rider who is well used to riding successfully in such a bit. Compare this horse's expression with that of the horse in the photo on page 14, top right.

BELOW: A simple eggbutt snaffle and grakle noseband. This horse is wearing a breastplate but no martingale.

stuck his ears in my mouth and away he went. Our first trip around Badminton in 1982 was out of full control most of the time. Later I learnt that he did not like the discomfort of a metal snaffle and he settled better in a vulcanite one. He became increasingly easier to control as he became more experienced and more confident in himself and in me.

Village Gossip was as near a runaway as makes no difference. I tried every kind of bit in his mouth. Without exception he was even stronger in any bit other than a metal eggbutt; the more severe the bit, the more he would fight – and with increased resolve.

Many horses, I feel, are overbitted and I am worried to see so many riders who have yet to gain a seat fully independent of their hands, riding in gags.

A gag is a specialised bit with which some horses and some riders perform well. To be able to ride with a gag is an acquired art and I have not yet found a horse that feels happy with me when I am riding in one. (See photo on page 14, top right.)

There are bits that suit certain horses, but most of the time, I believe, it is the style of riding that suits certain bits.

Some people hate martingales, feeling they are restrictive. Sometimes, possibly they are, and at moments if one is worn it is necessary to give the horse even more rein over a fence to compensate. I have been caught too often, however, trying not to wear a martingale on a horse that does fling his head up when

A twisted metal gag and American-style grakle noseband.

LEFT: *A 'bobbly' or Waterford bit with an English-style grakle noseband.*

ABOVE: *A simple, German loose-ring snaffle, cavesson noseband and no martingale.*

he is being restrained on the approach. Many do not do this and therefore do not need one, but a horse who does throw up his head can put himself in serious trouble if he does so just in front of an obstacle. (See 'Coffins' in Personal Reminders section.)

Horse Protection and Safety

Most front boots do not really protect the tendon from a heavy strike of the hind hoof or from the side edge of a front one. For years I have used Porter leg protectors, which are much lighter than boots and do not retain water. They comprise a double-thickness Plastazote wrap-around, moulded to the shape of the leg. Down the back of the tendon, a strip of impact-resisting polyethylene runs between the two layers of Plastazote.

These leg protectors have to be bandaged in place. Unless the bandage is pulled very tight it is difficult to harm the horse through bad bandaging, as there is a good thickness between the

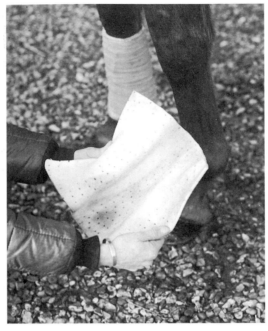

RIGHT: *A Porter leg protector.*

bandage and the leg. We use elasticated tail bandages for one-day events and Elastoplast for three-day events. The ends of bandages should be sewn. Taping bandages is a lazy way of securing them; not only can the tape come off, but more importantly, it can cause pressure rings on the leg, as the tape does not usually give as much as the bandage.

On the hind legs we use five-strap leather speedy-cut boots, lined with rubber. The leg protectors can be worn behind too, with the polyethylene strip running down the front of the cannon-bone. We have not found it necessary to use them thus on most of our horses.

Over-reach boots often do more harm than good. A horse can bring himself down by stepping on the skirt of one.

RIGHT SEQUENCE: *Bandaging the leg protector is not difficult. Maintain an even tension on the bandage and check that a finger can easily be fitted between protector and leg both around the joint and below the knee, once bandaging is completed.*

To secure, sewing is safer than tape. Temporarily held by a nappy pin, the end of the bandage is sewn down by over-stitches in each direction.

Separate safety stitches in the form of large X's are then sewn up and down the bandage to hold the layers and help prevent them slipping.

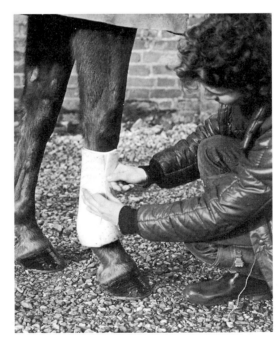

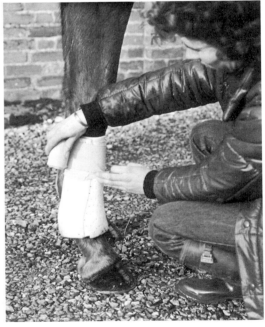

Without them a whole area of heel is exposed to the sharp toe of the back hoof, but I often wonder how much protection a piece of light rubber can offer: if the rubber was strong enough to deflect a serious blow, it would be too heavy for the horse to wear.

RIGHT: *Leather speedy-cut boots fitted with top and bottom straps a hole looser in order to avoid the edges of the boot causing a pressure ridge on the leg.*

FAR RIGHT: *Inner view of a speedy-cut boot.*

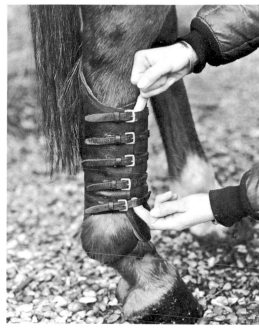

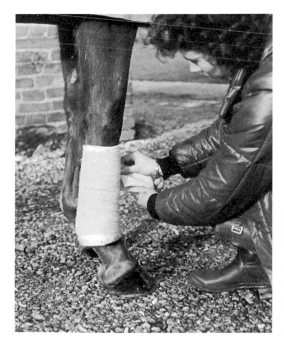

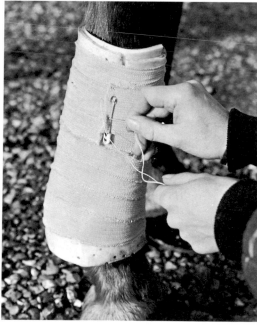

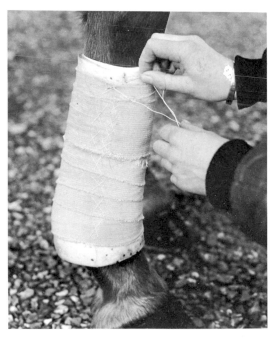

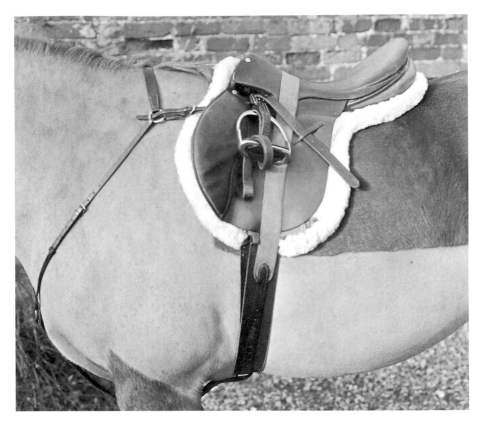

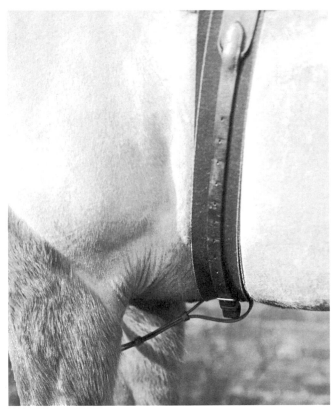

ABOVE LEFT: *A breastplate, surcingle, pair of racing girths and red-hide 'unbreakable' stirrup-leathers with stainless-steel irons.*

ABOVE RIGHT: *The webbing surcingle's buckle should be fitted centrally between the horse's forelegs. If it is a little to one side it may catch the horse behind his elbow, if it is higher up it will catch the rider's leg.*

A surcingle and a pair of racing girths are vital for safety. The former to help if the latter should break, although it would be very unlucky for both webbing girths to break at the same time. A breastplate is another essential item of tack.

All tack needs to be continuously checked for wear and tear. We change our competition pairs of racing girths (unelasticated, as elastic breaks without warning) and reins every three years.

It is wise to break in new tack at home before a competition, particularly new girth straps, nosebands and (red hide) stirrup leathers, as new leather has a habit of stretching considerably when it is first used.

All metal – buckles, stirrups and bits – should be of stainless steel, which breaks less frequently than nickel.

Bridles should be attached with a quick-release knot to a top plait in the mane by a shoe-lace. This prevents the rider taking the bridle with him if he flies over his horse's head.

Many people like the rest of the horse's mane unplaited for cross country. I prefer my horse's mane plaited to keep the hair out of the way when gathering

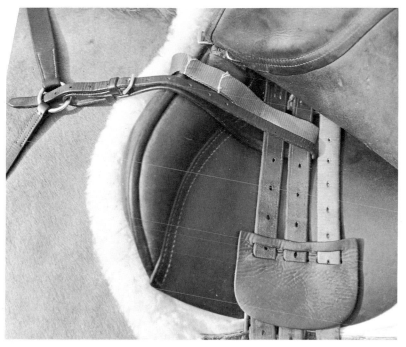 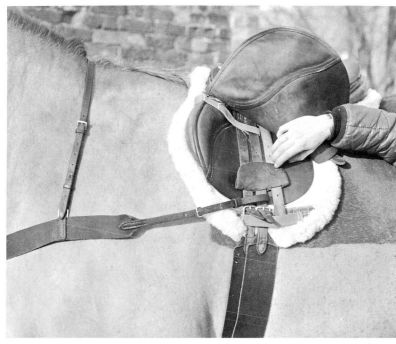

up the reins after a fence.

Studs on the outside of each hind foot are usually worn. We normally use the bigger studs with points on them. Front studs are put on only when the surface has become wet after a dry spell and it is then very slippery, or likewise if a thaw is in progress and the ground is wet on top but still hard underneath. The reason we do not habitually use front studs is twofold. Firstly, because the foot (apparently) always slips forward a little as it lands to lessen the impact of landing. If, indeed, a stud is doing what it is meant to do – prevent slipping – then the horse could become jarred if his front feet were never allowed to travel forward as nature intended. Secondly, there are two less

studs to make a hole in us if we find ourselves trampled upon.

Vaseline smeared down the fronts of all four legs sometimes helps the horse to slide over a fence rather than fall over it.

ABOVE LEFT: *A hunting breastplate attached by a specially lengthened strap to the girth straps. This avoids the risk of pulling out the D-rings of the saddle to which these breastplates are usually attached.*

ABOVE RIGHT: *The racing breastplate is attached differently and prevents the saddle slipping more effectively than the hunting breastplate. The pair of webbing racing girths is clearly seen in this photo. The girth guard helps prevent the buckles rubbing a hole in the saddle flap.*

Rider's Protection and Safety

The obligatory crash hat should be exchanged for a new one once it has suffered a heavy fall. The chin-strap should be adjusted comfortably but it must be firm. The draw string encircling the crown inside the hat must be adjusted so that when the rider hits his head on the ground his scalp cannot bang against the crown of the hat.

Back protectors and body protectors are becoming very fashionable and one day when the correct design has been fully tested and approved, they may become obligatory too.

Breeches with suede or leather inner-leg panels produce more grip when they are dry. However, in my experience, if it rains or the rider is splashed in a water-jump or, worse still, falls into it, attempting to ride with some types of leathered breeches can, on a leather saddle, be very difficult. For similar reasons leather gloves are hopeless across

country. Even the sweat on the horse's neck renders their grip virtually useless. String gloves are probably best. Resin (acquired from a sports shop) is useful, particularly if it is pouring with rain, to puff onto previously dampened insides of breeches and boots to help grip – or maybe it just helps morale?

Well-made waxed-calf-leather boots will protect a rider's leg in a fall better than will soft leather or rubber ones. It is much easier to ride with boots that come well up the leg and stop just under the knee. If a very high pair of boots is desired, it is necessary to ensure that the tops are cut down at the back of the boot or they will catch the rider behind the knee when he rides short.

It is safer to wear spurs if the horse is not sharp off the leg. A delayed reaction from the horse can cause trouble at a fence.

BELOW LEFT: *Leather gloves, or string gloves with leather fingers, are inadvisable as they slip when wet or when covered in sweat from the horse's neck.*

Neither of the whips shown is of great use. One is too bendy to have any effect and does not possess a knob on the top to prevent it slipping through the hand. The other is too short and hard. A wrist-loop is not required because there is often a necessity to change the whip quickly to the other hand.

BELOW RIGHT: *String gloves or wool/cotton gloves with rubber impregnations are probably the best type for cross country. The closer fitting they are to the hand, the easier they are to ride in.*

Both the whips shown are light but with the necessary amount of flexion. Both have martingale stops glued onto their ends to help the rider hold them. The short whip is useful on a nervous horse who objects to seeing a whip out of the corner of his eye.

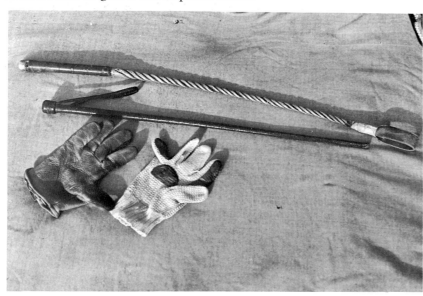

Fitness

An unfit rider or horse is a liability to safety.

If the rider does not ride a great deal, some extra activity will be needed to aid fitness. Squash, running, skipping – it does not really matter what is chosen so long as it makes the lungs and muscles work. I still find my wind is not good enough, even riding as much as I do, so I supplement my riding with skipping. I make a point of doing 300 skips every day, which takes only a few minutes, renders me breathless for a few more, and probably has its greatest impact on my mind. If I arrive at a point on a course when I start feeling too tired to make the required effort and begin to fear that I am not sufficiently fit, I hear a voice saying, 'Come on, you haven't done that hateful skipping every day for nothing – of course you are fit enough.' It works every time.

This rider ran the entire cross-country course of the Los Angeles Olympics for her fitness.

Interval Training

Many people have asked me to write about interval training but it is not a subject which can be written down comprehensively. Even attempting to put it on paper may be unwise. Horses are not machines, and although it is perfectly possible to give a breakdown of how a tractor can be made to work the same does not apply to making a horse fit. A little knowledge is a dangerous thing, but I dare not give more than an outline of the basic principle.

Following the initial six weeks of road work, schooling and the general beginnings of toning and hardening up, the programme can commence approximately seven or eight weeks before a three-day event. The objective is to enable a horse to reach his peak of fitness with the minimum amount of wear and tear. Accordingly training sessions, or work-outs, take place once every three or four days, gradually increasing the amount of canter work at each session. Apparently it takes between three and four days for a horse to fully recover from a work-out. To work a horse any sooner is to work a tired limb and invite injury; to work him later will benefit the horse correspondingly less as his muscles are beginning to slacken. If a horse is becoming too fit too soon, spacing the work-outs at five-, six- or even seven-day intervals will effectively slow up his progress.

The length of each of the three canters involved in each work-out and of the two intervening periods of relaxation and walking should be calculated to produce a horse almost fully recovered during the first break and half to threequarters recovered during the second. If he is asked to work again just before he has recovered he will thereby increasingly expand his heart and lung capacity thus building up his fitness in relation. This is a more logical approach than conventional fitness-training programmes which often involve pounding on in canter for twenty minutes or more at a time.

In 1974 when Bruce Davidson first introduced me to the system I worked from a pattern. Basically it began with three sessions of three-minute canters at 400 metres a minute interspersed with two three-minute breaks – 3 (3) 3 (3) 3 – and it built up over intervals of four days to three ten-minute canters at 400 metres a minute with two three-minute breaks between each – 10 (3) 10 (3) 10. It was only during the last three or four work-outs that any fast work was incorporated.

It is speed that kills. Galloping breaks down a horse quicker than any other work. During the last three or four work-outs of any training programme, four to five furlongs at a threequarter-speed gallop is about as much as I do.

Over the years I have come to appreciate how impossible it is to write a formula for fitness because every horse is different and requires slightly different work. It soon became evident that three lots of ten-minute canters involved too much hard work for my particular horses. The right amount depends on the type of horse, its temperament and the terrain being used. Flat terrain will require longer slow cantering than will hilly terrain. Hilly terrain is ideal for colder-blooded horses. In this case the three canters can be reduced to a total of maybe only seventeen or eighteen minutes.

These may be broken up into only two lots with accelerations uphill to keep the horse's incentive and interest. Fast work up not too steep an incline produces far less strain on the legs than it does when carried out on the flat. Also, less distance needs to be covered when galloping uphill. Occasionally a gallop on the flat is necessary though, because a horse needs to learn to re-adjust his balance depending on whether he is galloping on a gradient or not. If all his galloping is done uphill, he can find it rather difficult when he has to negotiate a flat steeplechase course at a competition. However, when canter work is carried out on hills, descents should be gradual and at an angle to lessen any jarring on the front legs. When the going is very hard it is advisable to canter uphill or on the flat only.

The feeling required when developing a horse's fitness with slow canter work is the following: he must be pumping up against the hand and flexing his muscles every stride, not lolloping along.

Some horses will respond better to a programme wherein the number of minutes they canter in any one bout never exceeds about six, but instead the speed is gradually increased. A useful programme can be worked out whereby the last minute of the second and third canters can be increased to 500 metres per minute and 600 metres per minute

respectively, starting approximately eight work-outs before the three-day-event. This routine can be continued until the speed of the final minute of each of the last two canters has increased to 550 metres per minute and 650 metres per minute respectively.

From twelve to fourteen work-outs overall normally proves enough.

NB: The intervening days are taken up with mostly hacking and/or schooling. The day after each work-out should always be devoted either to a long walk or to resting.

Once the horse has completed about six weeks of road work and general toning up, an interval training programme can begin.

Walking a Course

Walking a course is a science and an art in itself. It needs to be studied as thoroughly as riding.

Courses need much familiarising through study and thought. Every time I walk the same course, I notice something I had previously missed.

In a three-day event there is usually time to walk the cross-country course three times. I look upon the first walk as the most important. The first time a rider walks the course, he will be faced with the same view and share the same thoughts and queries that his horse probably will when he first sights the obstacle. In order to concentrate, absorb and retain these first impressions, it is necessary to make this first walk alone and undisturbed.

Having gained a general impression of the course, the rider needs to devote much longer to his second walk; in fact he should spend the most time on this part. Whilst walking round it is sometimes helpful to discuss the problems with others and seek advice. It is easy, though, to catch other people's neurosis about a fence that hitherto had not been a personal worry.

It is important to try and foresee all the potential problems that each fence might present. Although it may seem negative to think in this way, it does give the rider an advantage if he can file into his mental computer the possibilities of trouble and the action he would take.

It is very necessary to be equally

It is necessary to walk exactly the route the rider intends to take.

familiar with all the routes through each fence offering alternatives. However much a particular way does not appeal it is vital to know it, because it may transpire that that route is the only safe path through the fence.

In order to be accurate on lines into fences, it is useful to line up a mark on the fence with something on the other side.

Great attention should be given, all the way round, to the state of the going, noting where it is liable to become holding or slippery, where it is rough or undulating, any of which may throw the horse out of balance. It is often worth jumping to one side of a fence as the majority of people seem to follow, like sheep, the tracks of the horses before them which have usually made the centre of the fence deep if the going is wet.

A rider must watch for changes of light and shade and whether or not he will be riding directly into the sun. Horses find it as hard as people do to focus in changing light or glare.

In three-day events the rider must pay attention to the whereabouts of the penalty zones. It is so easy to be awarded a technical refusal for crossing in and out of a zone before the entire fence is negotiated.

On the final walk round, the rider should try to tread exactly the path he hopes to ride on his horse, making sure that the line into each fence is correct. A rider may work out an intricate line through a difficult combination using landmarks to help accuracy, only to discover, too late, as he gallops towards

the fence, that the landmarks are not identifiable from the back of a horse or they have been obscured by crowds or parked cars.

Immediately before every cross-country course I ride, I make time to be alone for a few minutes so that I can shut my eyes and watch my own 'film' of the course. Every turn and bump, every fence with its possible alternative routes, passes across an imaginary screen. My horse and I are seemingly transporting a camera and so I see each fence as it comes up to us. All the time I am thinking how I will communicate to my horse what type of fence we are approaching: by means of regulating his speed, using more or less hand and leg to balance him right back onto his hocks, or merely to set him up, I try to indicate to him what he is about to face.

Once that 'film' has come to an end, it is wise to glance at a list of the obstacles in the programme to make sure it does not contain a fence that was not included on the 'screen'.

I have never timed myself across country in anything but three-day events, and in those, only during the last few years. To do well in a one-day event it is necessary to go as fast as you safely can. Much the same applies to a three-day event, but it is worth timing it as it is over twice the length of a one-day course and there is more time therefore to make amendments.

Many hours of course-walking, course contemplating and course technique are all to no avail unless the rider remembers the most important point of all: to go out there and ride every fence

Walking the course with a measuring wheel to ascertain distance markers for riders' reference.

as if his horse will refuse. No amount of technique and pre-thought can take the place of plain riding. As science seems to swamp us in so many aspects, it is as well to remember that without the ability 'to go out there and kick', hours, maybe years, of contemplation will be of no value whatsoever.

One of the wisest pieces of advice I

have had, came from my father following a vain attempt to regain Be Fair's Badminton crown in 1974. We had just suffered a beastly fall over the downhill 'S' fence, attempting the most difficult route. 'Never forget one thing: you are out there, first and foremost, to do a clear round not to astonish the crowds or the TV cameras.'

My father also had a knack of telling me at exactly the right time, a few moments before the start, when I would be feeling at my most sick and wondering why I did this sport, 'Don't forget to kick, and – don't forget – you do it for fun.'

Once those agonies of nerves can be swept aside with the approach of the first fence, riding across country at all levels does become fun. It is a challenge, sometimes of enormous proportions, to the solidity of the bond of mutual trust that has been built up over the time that horse and rider have been together. It is a truly thrilling feeling when a green four-year-old displays enough trust to negotiate a few two-foot-high fences; it is no more or no less exhilarating to negotiate Badminton, simply infinitely more nerve-racking.

Last-minute inspection of a troublesome fence is sometimes helpful.

PART 2

The rider needs to have the feeling that threequarters of the horse is in front of him as he approaches any fence. In this way he is in a position to counteract any negative tendencies the horse may have before the fence as well as to help him come off his forehand and engage his 'engine' (hind end).

A hundred yards or more before a fence the rider needs to set the horse up and prepare him. Setting up too late leaves the horse still not properly balanced for the fence; setting up too early wastes a few, possibly valuable, seconds but is the preferable error of the two.

Photos 1–4 – The horse is trying to veer left in *Photo 2*. By *Photo 3* it has already been possible to correct this, because the rider is sitting 'in behind' the horse.

Photos 5–7 – The seats of the riders are not so deep and their weight and balance are a little in front of the horse's movement. All three of these riders are riding much longer than the one above. Within reason, the more open the angle between thigh and calf, the less security there is in the seat and the more difficult it becomes to balance the horse at speed.

The Take-off

Photos 1-4 - The riders' weight is centrally distributed and they are folding well from the waist. In *Photos 1 and 2* the horse could be pulling because, although in good balance, the rider appears reluctant to give any rein.

Photo 5 - The rider is fractionally in front of his horse's movement (compare with *Photo 1*). He is not folding from the waist but pivoting on his knee instead. This leaves little weight in his lower leg and none in his heel. If his horse hits the fence or stumbles on landing it will be easy for him to fall off.

Photo 6 - The rider is secure and his weight well distributed. Although he has not folded from the waist he is not restricting the horse with his hands.

The Jump

These six photographs show entirely different positions of hand, leg and body over a fence. Except for the rider in *Photo 5*, all are doing the single most important thing: they are giving their horses the freedom of rein to use themselves during the jump.

The positions demonstrated in *Photos 1, 2 and 3* offer the most secure feeling.

Photo 1 – One of those rare occasions when the rider's balance and weight is completely central. The hands have dropped down the neck, maintaining the required straight line from elbow through hand to bit. If that line is broken there is less flexibility in the arm and therefore in the contact.

Photo 2 – The rider is a little too upright, but essentially secure and giving his horse the freedom to jump.

Photo 3 – The rider is a fraction too far forward; if the horse should hit the fence or land badly, the rider has less chance of staying on than those in *Photos 1 and 2*. The contact line from elbow to bit is broken, offering less elasticity of contact.

Photo 4 – This rider is demonstrating survival of a very awkward moment. Neither looks comfortable, but the horse has the freedom of his neck to extricate himself, whilst the rider is using his natural balance and calf muscles to stay on board.

Photo 5 – Another awkward moment. The rider is endeavouring to turn her horse for the next element. For whatever reasons she has been unable to give him the freedom of rein.

Photo 6 – The rider's lower leg is not carrying any weight and supporting her. It is therefore not in a position to help her survive should trouble occur. The contact line is broken here too.

The Jump (cont.)

Both horses have dropped a foreleg in front of the fence, producing an unseating jump.

These photos ably demonstrate the importance of not pivoting on the knee and of distributing the weight through the lower leg and into the foot. They also show the necessity of the rider not being 'in front of the movement'.

Provided the freedom of the horse's head and neck is never impeded, it is an infinitely lesser sin for a rider to be 'left behind' than to 'go early'.

Photos 1–2 – Arm outstretched to aid his own balance, the rider is not interfering with the horse's mouth, but the second they have landed he is quick to regain his lost rein contact and readjust his balance.

Photos 3–4 – The rider has no support or security from his lower leg, instead he props himself up with his right hand on the horse's neck. If the horse had pecked he could have gone over his head.

Photos 5–6 – The lower leg is forming the support to the body, although the foot could be further through (home) in the stirrup for extra security. The fingers are open on landing, enabling the horse to have as much freedom of his neck as he requires.

Photos 7–8 – If the rider had not leant back over this big ditch and drop, she would have found it difficult not to fall off, as her horse crumpled on landing.

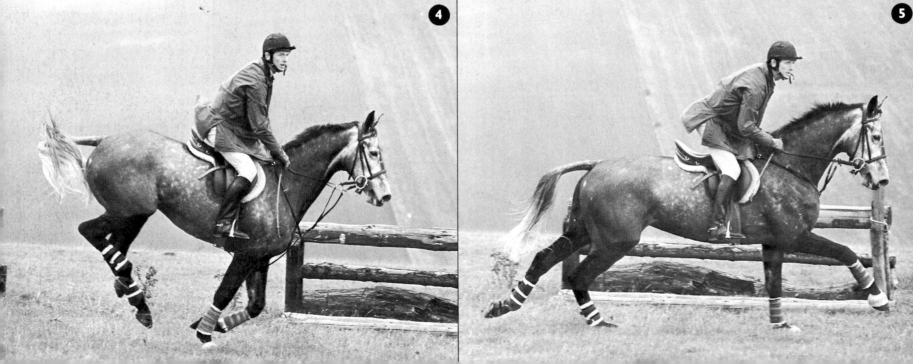

Control after a fence is equally as important as before it. Certainly in show-jumping, where the fences are in close proximity, the next fence is won or lost as the horse lands over the previous one.

If the contact has been slipped over the fence it needs to be regained as quickly as possible. Then is the moment for the rider to thank his horse if he did well. A pat or a good word helps the morale of both horse and rider.

Apart from needing a contact to indicate direction, most horses prefer to gallop feeling the contact. It helps balance them as does the correctly distributed weight of the rider.

A horse that canters and gallops in balance will tire less, have more chance of not straining a muscle or a tendon and be in a better position to jump.

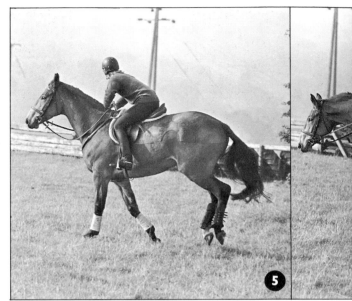

Photos 1-2 – A quick and balanced pick-up after landing. The weight is still firmly distributed down the leg into the foot.

Photos 3-5 – Much too slow to regain the contact.

Photos 6-7 – A little slow to pick up the contact. The rider seems to have 'missed' while picking up the left rein.

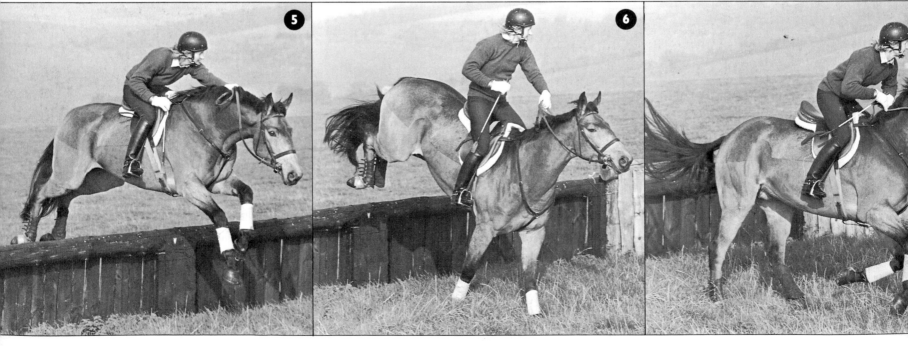

The whip is a necessary aid. In an emergency it can sharpen a horse's reactions and help him avoid a pending problem. It is very important to be able to use a whip, and to use it in either hand without dropping the reins.

More often than not, the whip is used as an encouragement, a means of assurance when, at the last second, the horse doubts himself or the fence.

Photos 1-8 – There is a ditch in front of the fence and this young horse lost his impulsion when he saw it. If no extra aid had been given at that moment the horse would have continued to lose impulsion. He would have arrived in front of the fence and either stopped or had to climb over without the aid of any forward impetus, thus leaving an uncomfortable experience in his mind.

APPROACH: **Usually not too fast. A horse often finds an upright more difficult to judge than a spread fence, which fills the eye better.**

A broken line of contact from elbow through hand to the bit does not offer the elasticity that the straight line of contact gives the horse.

Parallel

APPROACH: **Strong, on an increasing but held-together stride.**

Both these riders are in trouble. They would be more secure if they had less weight in their knee and more down through their lower leg and into the stirrup.

Photos 1–3 – Maybe this approach was not strong enough or perhaps the horse backed off when he sighted the ditch. The rider is not interfering with the horse's efforts to recover; he slips his reins, and keeps his balance and his weight off the front of the horse.

Photos 4–5 – The horse has stood off, maybe without sufficient impulsion, and the rider has taken evasive action in case the horse does not quite make the other side.

Double Combination

1

2

3

APPROACH: **Depends on the distance between the elements. In principle not too fast – the horse needs time to see what he has to do.**

Photos 1–6 – The balance and weight of the rider is central to the horse throughout. The weight is firmly distributed through the lower leg and into the foot. There is a straight line from the elbow through the hands to the bit at all times, except when the reins are being gathered up as the combination is completed. The horse is trying to veer off line to the left over the

7

8

9

first fence and so the fingers are unable to open and give quite as much freedom as they can over the next element.

Photos 7–12 – The rider is not really secure through his lower leg and into his foot. This makes it difficult for him to stay in balance with the horse and as a result he has crept a little in front of the horse's movement. No harm has come, but if the horse should stumble or attempt to run out or refuse then the rider is not in a position to be able to counteract these problems.

Double Combination (cont.)

Photos 1–4 – The rider seems to be riding too long and therefore finds it more difficult to sit up and be 'in behind' the horse. She is having to support herself a little on her hands.

Photos 5–8 – The horse is spooking at the second element and veering to the left. The rider is able to straighten him up as she has adopted the base of a secure lower leg and is not leaning too far forward.

Double Combination (cont.)

The young horse in this sequence is trying to veer left and miss the second element. The rider has a secure lower leg and consequently is in sufficient balance to take early corrective action.

Photos 3 and 4 portray an 'open rein,' which greatly aids direction. However, there are times when such action will inevitably impede the complete freedom of the horse's neck and head. The horse

will soon learn that if he keeps straight it is comfortable; if he does not, it is uncomfortable.

Bounce Fence

APPROACH: **A base of a short, bouncy canter with ample impulsion is needed. The distance between the elements dictates how strong this pace should be.**

Photos 1–3 – The rider is in good balance with her horse throughout the bounce. She is staying 'in behind him', and is in a position to be able to deal with any attempt the horse may make to refuse or run out, as well as being secure should he hit the fence or otherwise falter.

Photos 4–6 – The rider is supporting herself more on her hands than through the security of her seat and legs. In consequence she is not in such a good position to deal with any problems the horse may present.

Bounce Fence (cont.)

The rider in this sequence is in the centre of balance throughout, though for extra security there could be more weight in the heel in *Photos 1, 2 and 5*.

The horse has the necessary amount of freedom at all times and leaves the fence in as good a balance as he approached it.

APPROACH: **There is a short, steep rising bank before this fence. Because of that and the extremely wide fence out, it is necessary to approach this with more pace than a normal bounce, but still maintaining the roundness of stride and togetherness of the horse.**

The landing position of the rider in *Photo 7* is more secure than that in *Photo 3*, but the rider in the lower sequence has kept a locked elbow and not given the horse as much freedom as the rider in the top sequence.

Rail and Ditch

Two very green horses being introduced to a rail over a ditch.

Both riders have allowed their horses their heads to look at the obstacle and to give them the freedom to jump. But neither rider has allowed the rein to become actually loose until after the horse has taken off, lest he should take advantage and duck out. Both horses have been encouraged to take heart with a reminder from the whip. It is no good waiting for a young horse to refuse and then decide to be more positive – he will learn very quickly that he can stop. If the rider feels him question, then encouragement, as opposed to punishment, is a necessary option.

The riders here are producing some unorthodox styles resulting from the stop-go, staccato reactions of their horses. At the same time neither rider is in front of the movement and neither is impeding the horse's freedom to use himself as he wishes in order to jump.

Trakehner

APPROACH: **A strong, not too long canter as the horse will probably want to shorten when he suddenly sights the ditch.**

The horse is surprised by this fence and possibly needs more persuasion than he is receiving, as he backs off suddenly and quickly loses impulsion.

Having been in an urging position, the rider is left behind but is still allowing the horse full freedom as the hands drop either side of the neck in *Photo 5* and the fingers open up in *Photo 6* to allow the reins to slip through.

Trakehner (cont.)

Even though the lower legs of the riders are at a different angle on descent, both these sequences portray security and balance of the rider and freedom for the horse.

Ditch and Palisade

In the end, it is all about survival ...
The horse has his hindlegs caught on the fence; the rider has no security from his lower leg. The rider survives through balance and from support with his hands on the horse's neck, which fortunately did not duck down.

Coffin

APPROACH: **A short, bouncy canter with the horse's 'engine' (hind end) well engaged. The pace needs to be short and slow in order that the horse has the time to see that there is room to land over the fence before the ditch. However, THE SLOWER THE PACE THE MORE STRONGLY THE RIDER MUST USE HIS LEGS.**

Photos 1-2 – The rider is well balanced and ready for any spooking the horse may do at the ditch. She has let her reins slip as she jumped the first element to give the horse his freedom and still remain in the centre of balance. However, she has compensated by pulling her elbows out in order to take up the slack of the rein and keep the horse straight for the third element.

Photos 3-4 – The rider is a little too far forward. Instead of leaping boldly over the ditch her horse has popped in an extra stride, which she did not expect. If the horse wanted to opt out, the rider is not in a position to prevent him.

Photo 5 – A picture of stubbornness. This horse does not look scared or worried about the ditch. The rider is in a good position to do something about this. A few good kicks and probably one or two reminders from the whip and he should step over. At a fence of this dimension it is usually better not to turn away to re-approach.

The approach to this first element is uphill, the horse cannot see through it, and it is only as he arrives in front of the fence that he sees the ground runs away on the landing side and that there is a ditch on the far side as well.

If the horse is ridden in too fast, he will not have time to see that there is room to land between the fence and the ditch and that he is not being asked to jump directly into the ditch.

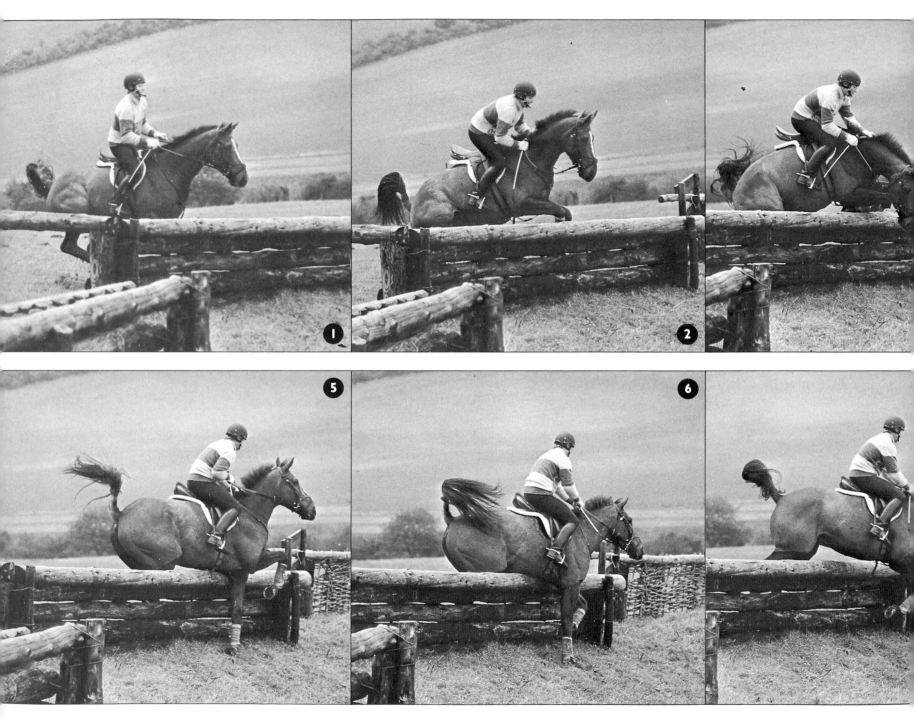

The approach was slow enough but the horse's 'engine' had not been gathered sufficiently well under him. When he saw the ditch he tried to refuse the first element at the very last second, after he had in fact taken off.

If the rider had been 'in front' of the horse on approach and take-off, the horse would probably not have reached the other side.

However, in *Photo 2* the sudden reversal of the horse's movement has thrown the rider slightly 'in front' of the horse at this point.

Here the horse seen on the previous two pages is re-presented at the same fence. He is still unsure of the ditch, as *Photos 3 and 4* portray, and the rider has failed to keep behind the movement when the

horse balks at the ditch.

Owing to the decrease in forward movement in front of the ditch, the rider has to sit down and really drive as they land over it (*Photo 8*), in order to make

the next stride long enough to reach the final element.

Photos 10 and 11 show the rider has been unable to catch up with the movement following the extra drive

needed. The arms and fingers are still offering the horse all the freedom he requires.

Coffin (cont.)

Photos 1-3 – The rider is a little too forward jumping in, but quickly rights herself to a position of balance to drive her horse out and give him his head.

Photos 4-6 – The rider's lower leg is not giving him the help he needs. Pivoting on the knee leaves the rider in trouble when the horse stumbles or, as in this case, jumps into the ditch instead of across it.

Sunken Road

APPROACH: **Similar to the approach for the coffin: a base of a short, bouncy canter with ample impulsion. The distance between the first two elements dictates how strong this pace should be.**

A young horse jumping his first sunken road. He is asked to approach it in trot in order to give him time to see what is ahead and work out what he has to do.

All the way through this sequence, the rider is in a position to counteract any negative moves by the horse, at the same time allowing the horse complete freedom of the rein. However, a loose

flapping rein, as in *Photo* 6, is
unnecessary and can lead to problems of
the horse running out.

Although few horses appreciate a tight
hold on their mouths over a fence, the
majority of horses seem to feel more
secure with a light contact on the reins
over a fence.

The same fence as on the previous two pages and a similar approach on a young horse.

This horse tries to veer left on landing over the first element when he fully sights the drop down into the road.

The action of the fingers and elbows is interesting throughout. Freedom is being given to the horse but the rider is making a greater effort to retain a more constant contact than in the previous sequence.

Following a very slow, bouncy approach, as the rails are so near the drop down into the road (about three yards apart), the rider has failed to create sufficient impulsion and the horse has found it quite a struggle to jump out.

Even though the rider has been 'left behind' at the final element, the horse still has all the freedom he needs from the reins.

Whatever happens to the rider over a fence, the two really important points are:

1. He stays on board.
2. He gives his horse freedom to use himself.

A young horse faces his first bigger bank, still out of trot. He is uncertain and veers left. The rider's left heel and right rein counteract this from a centrally balanced, upright and secure

position.

Plenty of rein is given although the rider is 'left behind' in *Photos 7 and 8*. Once it has been necessary to be 'in behind the horse' and use considerable

push, it is often difficult immediately to catch up with the movement again. This does not really matter provided the horse's freedom is not impeded by pulling on the reins as the rider is left

behind.

In *Photo 5* the hind hoof is precariously near the front tendon. Leg protection is a wise precaution.

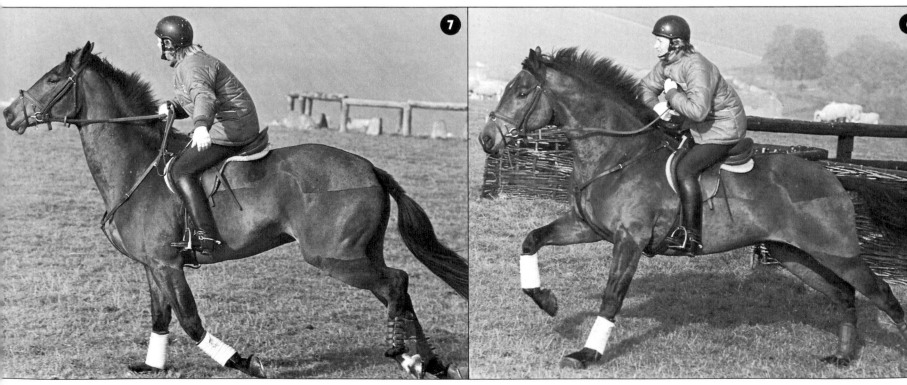

This young horse has trotted up a slope and found a sleeper drop at the summit. He needs time to work it all out.

The rider is allowing him all the rein he wants to stretch down and look at the problem afoot, but at the same time she is not leaning up his neck and is ready to coax him over the edge if he should need it.

Photos 5–7 show the gathering up of slipped reins.

Landing into the Face of a Bank

APPROACH: **A bouncy stride with the horse well on his hocks to encourage him to land lightly over the fence. A long, flat stride on the approach will encourage a horse to land heavily on the bank and possibly to crumple.**

Photo 1 – The horse has popped sensibly over the rail onto the bank.

Photo 2 – The horse has jumped big onto the bank and the rider has adopted the necessary position to withstand the jar of the landing.

Photos 3–4 – The bank is not clearly defined. This horse failed to comprehend what type of fence it was. It is necessary to approach this fence fairly slowly in order to give the horse time to understand.

Irish Bank

APPROACH: **Reasonably strong but not long and flat.**

Photos 1–5 – Although the lower leg has lost its security (and its stirrup) and is swinging back, the rider is still allowing the horse to use his head and neck.

Photos 6–8 – This rider has much more security through his lower leg and foot. The horse is being a little restricted by the hand. This is probably because the bank is much smaller than the one in the sequence above, and the rider is restricting the horse purposefully to ensure he does not attempt to clear the whole bank without touching down on it.

Photo 9 – The rider is too far forward and not in a secure position to deal with any stumbling that may occur on landing.

Different Types of Bank

APPROACH: **Reasonably strong but not long and flat.**

Both these sequences show a good and secure balance between horse and rider.

Photos 1-4 – A 'pillbox' being negotiated. In *Photo 2* both the horse's hindlegs are flat on the fence. Athleticism in the horse is of great importance.

Photos 5-7 – A bridge-type bank. There is no filling underneath this fence and only a horse who has been trained with care through the grades would have the confidence and knowledge to know what to do with such an obstacle.

In *Photo 6* the right rein is opening and the rider's body leans slightly to begin to turn the horse in the air. In *Photo 7* the left-hand fingers are opening to allow the horse to turn.

Bank and Rail

APPROACH: **A round pace, not too fast with hind end well engaged.**

The horse veers a little to the right as he lands on the bank and is confronted not only by the rail but also by the drop four yards beyond.

The rider is in the centre of balance throughout. At times the toes are pointing down but the weight is essentially in the right place – down through the lower leg and foot.

In *Photos 7 and 8* the rider is not able

to give the horse full freedom of his head because he has to restrain him lest he jumps too far out and lands either on the edge of the bank-down or possibly even over the edge.

Bank and Rail (cont.)

Jumped in reverse, this obstacle has to be attacked a little more strongly as the horse has to jump out onto the bank and take off over the rails immediately he lands. On landing over the rails, he

has a stride to gather himself together before the descent.

In this sequence the rider has slipped the reins more noticeably than the rider in the previous sequence. This could

cause a problem if there was an awkward obstacle following in quick succession.

APPROACH: Stronger than most instincts of self-preservation dictate. A rounded, powerful stride with 'engine' well engaged is needed to encourage the horse to jump boldly onto the bank and be able to spring directly off again. A tepid approach may allow the horse to put in a shuffle on top of the bank. This will make the trajectory of the jump off the bank very steep and could encourage either a peck or a fall.

Photo 3 – The horse is clearly surprised to find the drop on the far side of the fence. This momentary hesitation could have been enough to throw the rider forward if he had not been in such a secure position (see *Photo 2*).

Hayrack with False Ground-line

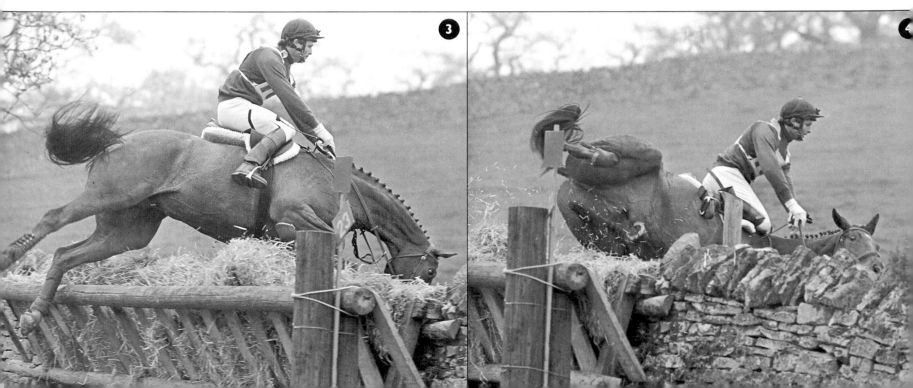

APPROACH: **A difficult fence for a horse to judge. A rounded, shortening stride with a strong leg. A flat, long stride will make it difficult for the horse to correct himself if he has misjudged the fence.**

The ground-line is false, being placed in under the near-side top of the fence. If, as it is believed usually happens, the horse judges the fence from the ground-line, it would be easy for him to hit the fence.

Angling false ground-lines is a risk. If the fence is misjudged and hit, the horse is more likely to overturn if he hits it on an angle than if he hits it straight on. This applies to hitting any obstacle.

Photo 1 – This horse finds no problem on the angle.

Photo 2 – This horse hits it hard and looks in trouble.

Photos 3–4 – This fence was approached straight but the horse and rider *are* in trouble.

Drop Fence

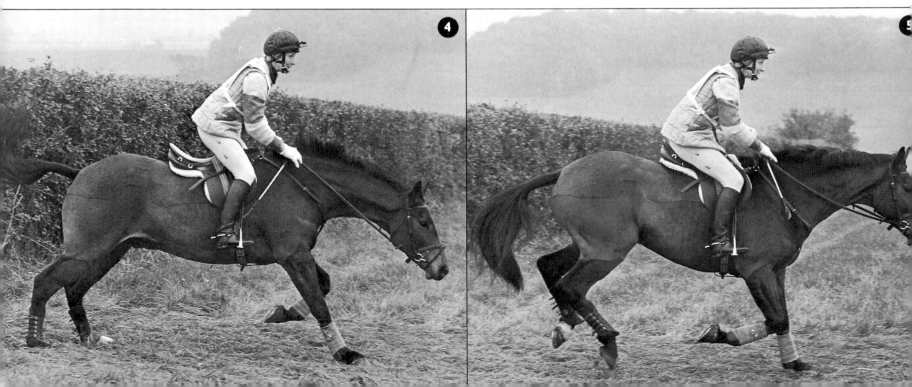

APPROACH: Not too fast, but on a lengthening stride to encourage the horse to jump out and not drop down too vertically which might cause him to topple over more easily.

A young horse meets his first drop fence.

In *Photo 1* the horse's face shows some surprise at the unexpected disappearance of his landing spot.

It is rarely worth trying to make a horse stand off at a fence where he cannot see the landing. More than likely he will want to drop in a short stride to check that there is in fact a safe landing on the other side.

This sequence portrays just how much a horse needs to use his head and neck at each different part of the jump. Neither is in the same position in any of the six frames. The rider's opening fingers allow this freedom.

Drop Fence into Combination

APPROACH: **Not too fast and on a slightly lengthening stride unless the distance between the elements is short. Shortening into a drop can cause too steep a trajectory on landing.**

The rider's balance and weight distribution are good.

In *Photo 4* the fingers have opened to allow the horse freedom and the rider is sitting back to counteract the jarring effect of landing over a drop.

In *Photo 6* the rider has drawn back her elbows and kept an upright body in order to maintain contact with the horse's mouth. Without impeding the horse's freedom this enabled her to correct any slight deviation in steering or any tendency to lurch onto the forehand, that may have occurred between the two elements.

Rail Across Open Water

APPROACH TO ANGLED RAIL: **A strong, increasing stride but not as fast as for open water as a greater degree of accuracy is needed in order to jump the fence at its most assailable point.**

In *Photo 1* the rider is in balance with the horse. She appears to be slightly leaning on her forearm which prevents a fully elastic contact. This could be because the horse is a puller.

In *Photo 2* the rider has opted to stay in behind the movement lest the horse pecks on landing. She has slipped her reins but possibly could have released them even further for full freedom of the horse's head and neck.

APPROACH TO STRAIGHT RAIL: **Attack at an increasing speed having set the horse up at least a hundred yards before the fence.**

In *Photos 3 and 4* both riders have been left behind on take off but have given sufficiently with their contact. The rider in *Photo 3* must be giving by opening her fingers because the elbow looks locked. In *Photo 4* the rider is giving by releasing her elbow.

Open Ditch

APPROACH: **Attack at an increasing speed but the horse still needs to be set up and prepared at least a hundred yards before the fence. The setting-up is particularly important because sometimes a horse does not sight a hole in the ground until very late.**

In *Photos 1–3* the rider had not accelerated enough into the fence and the horse does not clear the ditch. The rider takes evasive action with seat and legs but still allows the horse freedom to extricate himself from trouble.

Photo 4 illustrates the same fence viewed from the other side. The approach was stronger and the horse is jumping bigger.

Unfinished Bridge

APPROACH: **Attack at an increasing speed, having set the horse up about a hundred yards earlier.**

The sequence shows the rider leaning well back. He still has a secure hold on the reins although he has already slipped them to enable him to lean back.

It is sometimes believed that by holding onto the horse's mouth as he lands over a drop, the rider will keep the horse's head up and prevent him falling over. The horse's strength is infinitely greater than the rider's, and whilst it is possible to precipitate a fall by hindering the horse's recovery through being in the wrong balance, it is doubtful whether a rider can prevent one that is actually about to happen.

In *Photo 3*, despite the hold on the reins, the horse has managed to drop his head, which he needed to do in order to regain his balance and his legs. The jar of the landing has jerked the rider out of the saddle but he looks in no danger of evacuating as his weight distribution and balance are good.

The rider shown landing over a similar fence in *Photo 4* is in good balance, security and harmony with the horse. The hands maintain a balancing contact but are not pulling at the mouth.

Spread and Drop

APPROACH: **Attack at an increasing speed.**

These fences, fortunately, are uncommon as they are not generally believed to be very safe. A horse can spread himself over the parallel and then, on seeing the drop, may begin the descent before his front legs have cleared the back rail. This type of fence therefore needs to be approached at a faster speed than that normally used for an upright rail and drop.

Photos 1–4 – The rider is keeping an entirely central position through good weight distribution, balance and sheer strength of leg and back. This forward seat makes it less necessary to slip the reins. In *Photo 2* the horse is slightly hollowing against the contact, but thereafter the straightening of the elbow gives the horse sufficient length of rein.

Photos 5–7 – The same fence negotiated equally successfully by balance alone.

Wall and Drop

APPROACH: **Slow, bouncy canter; very strong leg.**

The horse is unable to see where he can land until just as he takes off. Some horses think it might be safer to bank the wall to give themselves time to see what is on the other side. This can be very unseating for the rider and unbalancing for the horse.

Horse and rider seem undaunted by the results of banking this wall – both continued over the next elements of the quarry without any trouble.

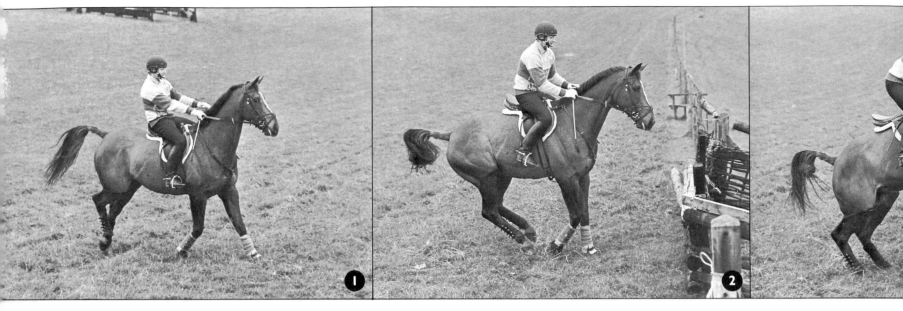

APPROACH: **Bouncy and short striding. Do not ask for a stand-off as the horse cannot see the landing and is therefore unlikely to want to stand back.**

The horse is not sure about this and needs some serious urging.

Photos 3 and 4 show the horse not being allowed quite as much rein as he would like. In order to try and indicate to the horse that he is not to go bounding down the slope on a great long stride, after he has jumped, such an inhibition is sometimes necessary.

APPROACH: A short, bouncy canter – usually best to stand off.

The horse momentarily considers slipping to the right before take-off. The correction of left hand and right leg is accepted and the horse jumps off the bank reasonably straight.

Fence at Bottom of Downhill Slope (cont.)

The sequences show two entirely different styles. Both are balanced and both are allowing their horses to use themselves.

The rider in the second sequence appears less secure, but she has an amazing natural balance to which orthodox style sometimes means little. This rider is also holding her right rein in a different grip to her left one.

In *Photo 7* the rider is sitting up, giving her horse his freedom and trying to keep out of trouble, but things have gone wrong on take-off and they are going to fall.

APPROACH: Very slow canter, probably breaking into a slow but strong trot in the last few strides – and not forgetting to keep kicking when in trot.

Both these sequences indicate how much a horse needs the use of his head and neck. Both riders are allowing their horses full freedom, whilst ensuring they themselves stay out of trouble.

Landing on slopes, as in these photos, is much less jarring and therefore exerts less strain on a horse than when landing on flat or, worse still, rising ground.

Ski-jump

APPROACH: **Very slow trot, but with a strong leg.**

The horse and rider can only see the tops of the surrounding trees as they climb the ramp towards the fence. The horse has to take off out of trust alone as he cannot see where he is going to land until he has begun his trajectory.

A slow approach is necessary in order that the horse will jump as small and neatly as possible and thereby land in balance on the very steep downhill slope that follows.

The narrow 'funnel' fence only a few yards from the base of the ski-jump shown, quickly discovers those not in full balance and control.

Photos 6-8 – Hardly in control.

Note: The abundance of grease seen on the front of the horse's legs is applied to help them slide out of trouble.

Bank-drop and Bounce

APPROACH: **By virtue of the jump onto the bank, this fence has to be ridden with attack but in a canter that is as round and controlled as possible.**

Once again great strength of leg as well as good balance enables this rider to stay with the movements of his horse without leaning back.

Only two strides later they have to negotiate a high bounce fence whose elements are about five yards apart.

The rider has not slipped his reins but because of the forward seat, his elbows can do the giving. The horse has freedom of his head and neck and the rider continues to maintain a balancing contact with the mouth throughout.

Steps Down

1

2

6

7

APPROACH: **Short, bouncy canter. Sometimes trot.**

A young horse finding the way down a staircase for the first time.

The rider stays central, ready for any questions the horse may ask. At the same time the horse has complete freedom to stretch, look and jump (see particularly *Photo 4*).

Steps Down (cont.)

Three different weight distributions of the rider.

In *Photos 4 and 5* the rider changes very quickly from being too far forward to too far back.

There is another fence very close to the base of the steps on a sharp turn to the right which would account for the rider in *Photo 5* using his weight and strength against his horse to try to steady and turn him. Possibly he would not have had to take such drastic action if he had sat back, with his horse better balanced and more on his hocks when descending the penultimate step.

Steps Up

APPROACH: **Strong, but not flat or fast. The horse needs to have his hind end well under him and be in a round and attacking rhythm. If he comes in without sufficient controlled power, he will find each step up an increasing struggle.**

Photos 1–2 and 5–6 – Both riders are keeping up their horses' revs by being 'in behind' them.

Photo 3 – The rider was maybe tempted to turn in to these steps too sharply, and the horse did not have time to work out what he had to do.

Photo 4 – Now that he understands, the horse jumps up well.

APPROACH: However simple the fence, it is wise not to be on a long flat or fast stride on the approach.

An elevated landing meets the horse much quicker than he is expecting and sometimes he does not unfold his legs in time before the landing hits them.

Fence into Water

Most young horses are naturally wary of water. Once they have learnt to trust it they usually thoroughly enjoy jumping into it.

When introducing a horse to water it is vital that the bottom of it is sound and will not frighten or hurt him by giving way or having sharp protrusions in it.

Before actually asking the horse to jump in, it is best to allow him to paddle first to familiarise him with the strange, shiny and noisy surface.

The early fences into water should be of a size that the horse could step over from a standstill should he stop. Once a horse, young or otherwise, turns his back on a fence he is a step nearer learning how to become a stopper. From the very beginning a cross-country horse must learn that he never turns away. No matter what, he must somehow arrive on the other side of the fence.

APPROACH: **Short, bouncy canter or trot; strong leg.**

The rider is in a good balanced position which has enabled her to urge her somewhat suspicious novice horse through a fairly testing water complex. There is barely room to land between the rails and the edge of the water. At this sort of fence, many novices would prefer to stop because they think they are being asked to jump over the rails directly into the water.

The sense of achievement for both horse and rider when a fence has been negotiated is very real.

Drop Fence into Water

APPROACH: Owing to a wide stretch of open water that has to be cleared only a few strides earlier, this fence has to be approached on a reasonably strong but holding stride.

Photos 1-4 – The horse has made a sensible, economical jump in, and the rider is in good balance. The jump out is no problem.

Photos 5-7 – The horse has jumped in quite extravagantly and the rider is taking suitable evasive action to deal with the sudden reduction in motion experienced on hitting the holding effect of the water.

This horse loves water, almost too much for his own good. He is taking an over-extravagant leap in, despite having been brought in close to the fence, and despite the efforts of the rider to restrain him in the air.

The rider could have more weight down through the stirrup to help him counteract the inevitable whiplash action the body receives as the horse's motion is suddenly restricted on entering the water.

Recovery is quick and the fence out presents no problem.

Bounce and Drop into Water

APPROACH: **Short, bouncy canter, giving the horse time to see and work it all out, but with a very strong leg, lest his courage should suddenly fail him.**

A firm and secure seat throughout. The rider is sitting up and just a fraction behind the horse at times, prepared for any trouble and ready to rebalance.

In *Photo 7* the rider takes in a reef of rein with her left hand but has no time to shorten the other rein before the jump out.

In *Photos 10 and 11* both are already turning left for the next fence.

The rider is centrally balanced and very secure. The horse has all the rein he needs and more. He has been rebalanced in *Photos 3 and 4* and thereafter has seen his way out.

In *Photos 5, 6 and 7* both are already turning left for the next fence.

APPROACH: **A strong, bouncy canter, quietly increasing in the last couple of strides in order to try and produce a slightly flatter trajectory to enter the water.**

If a horse enters water over a big drop in a nearly vertical trajectory, he will probably turn over as he lands. The weight of the water will stop his front legs moving out quickly enough to take the next stride before his hind end, vertically above them, flips over.
In this sequence the horse bellies this fence which has the effect of ejecting the rider vertically upwards and jerking both reins out of her hands. Only enormous good fortune prevents the reins going right over the horse's head.

Further enormous fortune and a genuine horse enables the bounce fence out to be successfully negotiated too.

Fence in Water

APPROACH: These fences need to be ridden slowly but with a firm hand and leg to help hold the horse together. He can become sprawly from the drag of the water on his legs.

A pole just above the water is not an easy fence for a horse to judge or to understand. It is necessary somehow to ensure he actually takes off.

In *Photo 1* the rider is 'hailing a cab', a very useful balancing tactic in emergencies. It could be that the rider gave his horse some encouragement with his whip – often necessary to make the horse realise that the pole on the water really is a jump.

This rider is relying on the strength of the grip of his knee for security. His weight is not too far forward over the fence, but he is lacking support from his lower leg on landing.

His line of contact is good, allowing his fingers to open and give the horse what rein he needs.

This novel fence first appeared in the 1984 Olympics. It involved jumping from one level to another over a waterfall. It was in fact so small that virtually no horses took exception to it.

In *Photos 1 and 3* the rider's hands are unnecessarily high, otherwise the central balance and security are intact.

Bullfinch

APPROACH: **Strong but short stride.**

Unless well practised, the horse may either try to stop or clear the full height. The rider needs to hang on very tight. Not only does the motion of the jump suddenly slow up as the horse brushes through the bullfinch, but also bits of birch from the fence can sneak between the knee and the saddle and lever the rider out.

Photos 1–4 This horse tries to clear the top of a bullfinch and by so doing lands so far out that he is at the base of the ensuing bank. The rider is using great strength of leg and seat to stay on board rather than throwing his weight back.

In *Photo 5* the birch is pulling the rider's leg away from the saddle. (Note that the lower strap of the grakle has been mistakenly fastened above the bit instead of below it. This is easy to do and causes considerable pinching to the horse's mouth.)

Fence under Roof

APPROACH: **Slowly but with a strong leg to give the horse time to judge that there is room for his head if he jumps.**

If the roof is very high (as in *Photo 2*), then the horse may not notice it. If he does, he is liable to duck at the moment he is contemplating taking off (as in *Photo 1*). This can cause either a refusal or a fall.

APPROACH: **It is necessary to find exactly the right line. Normally it is best to divide the angle between the two rails and aim to jump that imaginary divider at right-angles.**

It is vital when walking the course to find the line you want and then look for a suitable spot on the fence and a landmark beyond, both of which must be easily identifiable from the back of a galloping horse.

It is usually easier to keep a straight line on a fence when accelerating into it. For this reason it is probably best to set the horse up and gather up his 'engine' some way back and then ride the pre-conceived line positively.

In both sequences the horse has his freedom over the fence and on landing.

The insecure lower leg of the rider in the bottom sequence is in sharp contrast to that of the rider above. There is never enough weight through his leg into his stirrup from the approach onwards, because he is using his knees to grip too much and not allowing the weight to be distributed any further down.

Table or Churn Stand

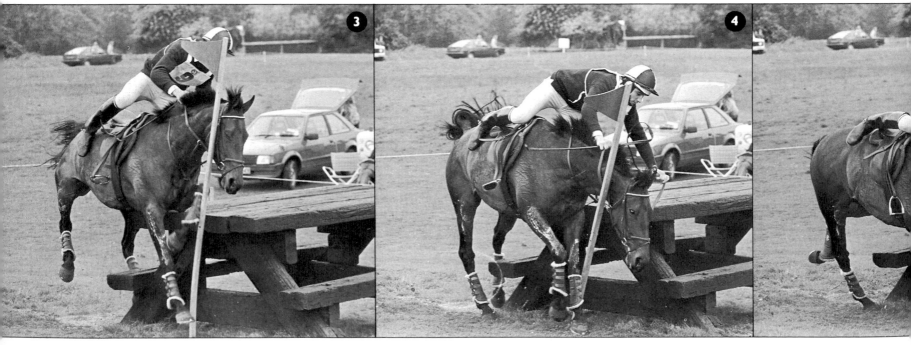

APPROACH: **Usually the ground-line of these types of fence is hard to judge, particularly if the table has no front to it. Therefore the approach needs to be strong but holding, so that if the horse misjudges he can easily put in a short stride.**

Photos 1 and 2 – Provided these types of fence are not too wide, angling them to save time is all right. If they are wide, it is better to be straight, as angling makes a spread bigger.

Photos 3–7 – Missed. The rider is wearing a stop-watch and was possibly chasing the clock. When his horse decided to try and avoid this very narrow island fence he found it quite easy to do so.

If a horse is liable to run out, he can use the strength that his speed creates against the rider's efforts to keep him straight. Therefore it is best to steady for narrow fences or places where a rider thinks his horse may duck out.

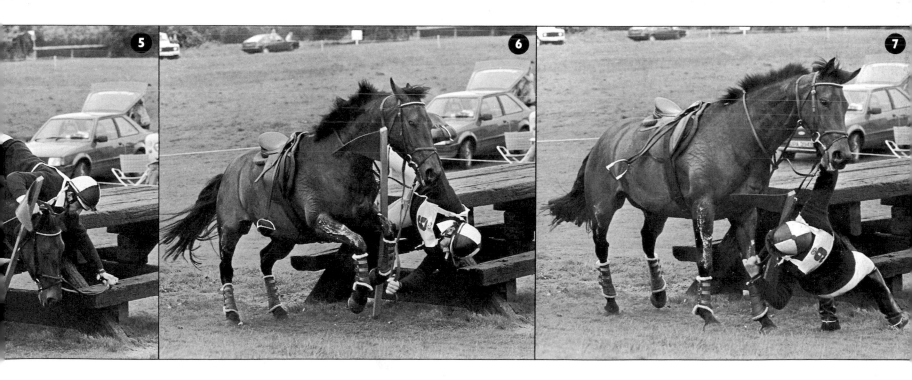

APPROACH: Strong, bearing in mind it is preferable not to stand off or the horse could have a very wide jump indeed. It is easy for a horse to misjudge the dimension of the spread, so it is best to encourage him to come reasonably close to the bottom rail by holding the contact firmer and squeezing more with the legs if he feels that he is about to take off a stride too soon.

Rail and Ditch in Shadow

APPROACH: **A particularly awkward fence to approach. It invited the rider to cut too tight around the turn into it, and then surprised the horse with a big ditch on the far side of the rails. This ditch was hard to see as the fence was in deep shadow out of bright sunlight. It is necessary to straighten for this fence some way back and then ride strongly but not too fast; this way the horse has time to re-focus from the light to dark and see what he has to jump.**

In this sequence the horse has misjudged and stood off a long way back. He was probably losing impulsion in the last few strides as he tried to distinguish what was in the shadows.

In *Photos 1 and 2* the rider is doing all he can to help, by giving the horse his head and keeping his weight off the horse's front end.

Both emerge unscathed.

Steeplechase Fence

APPROACH: **Apart from the initial re-balancing about a hundred yards away, this fence can be attacked at speed.**

The rider's weight distribution and balance are all right. The line of contact is broken, offering less elasticity of contact.

PART 3

Personal Reminders

The following are extracts from my 'Little Black Book', a sort of diary which I kept in the early seventies to record some of the things I had learned and some of the worst mistakes I had made.

Bouncing

"This used to be something you always prided yourself in doing well. You've forgotten that as Be Fair is so much stronger now you have got to be strong to the point of rough to get him into a bouncy stride. Once you have him under you, continue to apply the aids and keep him in the bounce until he has taken off. At Badminton '74 at the 'S' Fence, *without realising* it you allowed him to lengthen too much out of the turn and lost the bouncy stride you had achieved. Remember Osberton '73: you forced him over the coffin, through sheer strength, because you were so frightened that he would stop as he had done two fences previously. At the Quarry, Badminton '74 again he lengthened and flattened the last four strides: *you must notice this and contain it.*"

Lane Fences

"If you are jumping into a lane, down which you have to turn sharply either left or right, don't ask for a stand-off. He will not want to jump big if he sees he can't go straight on. If he does stand off, be prepared for him to land so short that he gets his front legs inside the far bar (if a spread) - sit back. However, have him full of impulsion, for he might rather not take off if he thinks there's no room to land."

Banks

"When jumping onto the face of banks, collect up a little; don't let him go headlong into it. If a little collected, he will land lightly.

Sleeper-faced banks - you cannot approach these very fast. You must take a pull (and give a kick) however easy they may look.

NB Punchestown, walled bank up onto a road. Looked quite easy but imposing and big, so you let him gallop on at it. Even going at that speed he contemplated putting in a short stride because he wasn't sure what it was. Then he made an awkward jump as though off three legs. So, take a pull, but EARLY enough to still have plenty of impulsion. This is an obstacle a horse rightly looks at.

However, at an ordinary medium-height Irish bank you can gallop at it with an increasing stride, because he's not going to skin himself on that, and you want him to jump cleanly off again."

Angled Combinations

"Make sure you are going slowly enough and are well up together. Twice you have made the mistake of not realising just how fast you were going until you tried to turn for the second/third elements, e.g. Windsor, Open Intermediate '71 (two uprights followed by a third, offset) and Badminton '72 (Tom Smith's Walls). Because Be Fair is a very agile horse you can forget that when on a long stride it still *must* take longer to turn. So, THINK AHEAD."

Short Cuts

"In a three-day event, don't take short-cuts near the beginning. Present the horse straight and fair at the first eight to ten fences, after which he will be going on and you can then begin to contemplate shorter, more difficult routes. But always ask yourself, 'Is it really worth it?' and also 'Is the most difficult way through a fence really the quickest?'

Badminton '72 - Dick Stillwell advised you to swing wide all through Huntsman's Close because it was early on, therefore it made it easy for the horse, facing no problem at short notice early on in the course."

Windiness

"If you are particularly windy of a fence, it is rarely a wise step to ride into it flailing your whip, and going faster and faster in order to overcome your own fear. The poor horse still has to jump it like any other fence, and if you behave in this way he will have a hard job.

NB Badminton '72, Normandy Bank. You hit him after the ski-jump, to say 'Watch it!' Then, because you knew you must jump big onto the bank because you were scared he might otherwise try to take a stride, you increased your speed, but you did it by free-wheeling and not by changing him down into third gear. Consequently he was flat and when he came in wrong he did not have his 'engine' under him to shorten up and jump powerfully. Instead he did a half-hop up onto the bank. Having lost much impulsion in so doing he only just managed to jump straight off again.

When there is a difficult fence, beat him some way off, if you must, to increase your own courage, but make a point of changing down into third gear and driving him up into a stronger contact."

Water

"You must always go slowly into water. Be Fair jumps much too big into it anyhow, and mustn't have the addition of speed to help him peck.

NB Cullompton, Novice '70: tiny jump in, but he still jumped huge. Windsor, Open Intermediate '71: he jumped in so big out of a bouncy canter, there was no time to make the required turn after it.

You must slow up in plenty of time, for he is much too inclined to say, 'I know about this; let me go.' You will have less chance of re-steadying him if you are pulling up too close to the fence.

At Punchestown you were still pulling up as you jumped into the sheep-wash. Luckily he steadied himself, got in a quick stride and jumped out, but by so shuffling he had lost his impulsion and you had to draw your stick to prevent him trying to put in a short second

stride into the following rail, which would most likely have ended in a crunch."

Hilltop Fences

"Fences that follow shortly after a rise have been the cause of your only two falls so far: Eridge, Novice '70 – small post and rails at the top of a hill; and Wylye, Open Championships '71 – wide open-fronted sleeper fence with false ground-line.

The horse will want a short breather when he reaches the summit but, FOR GOD'S SAKE, after two or three strides really kick him up into the bit; tell him something's coming and, with your *motor well underneath you*, sit still and *don't* ask him to stand off.

NB Wesel: at the Vicarage-Vee-type fence (corner of rails over a ditch) after a steep bank, came in wrong and only just made it, because you weren't tough enough in saying 'Come here' after the rise. DON'T FEEL SORRY FOR HIM BECAUSE HE'S CLIMBED A HILL, or you'll feel much sorrier for him once he's fallen.

Also Tidworth '71, hay-pile on top of hill (fourth last) – you didn't bother to push him up, he hit it – the only one he hit."

Trotting into Fences

"Always pull back in time so you can be increasing, even if only gently, with your 'motor' under you into the fence.

Tidworth '70, 4th fence: pulled back too late, consequently had no impulsion

over drop and only just made next two elements, which were small. Similar fault at palisades out of sunken road. Didn't have time to gather himself together – hit it hard.

Kyre, Novice '70 penultimate, rail across bottom of a deep dyke under trees: didn't have him really between you as he came over the brink of the dyke, consequently he wasn't balanced enough. When he found he was wrong it was difficult for him to shorten, so he swerved to the side to give himself extra room and was lucky to make it."

First Fences

"It is vital that you ride into the first and second fence in the manner in which you wish to attack the rest of the course. Because they are easier you are inclined to be far from positive about them. The first fence at Badminton '73, as compared to that of '72, influenced whole round.

Kiev: rode into first like a demon because you knew what fence two was, therefore had the most brilliant ride to date."

False Ground-lines

"However easy they look, whether they are situated in the middle of a long stretch of galloping and are consequently tempting to ignore, always, always take a pull – just to tell him to 'Watch it'.

NB Wylye, Novice '70, a small hayrack: galloped on at it and very nearly crunched."

Woods (dark and light)

"Fences in woods can be hard to see. Be Fair never properly saw the fence he fell over in Kiev. You were going too fast anyhow, but he would have got away with it had he been able to see. Take a pull, and jump them as if they are *tricky* however straightforward they may appear."

Drops

"Never ask for a stand-off when jumping a drop fence.

NB Sherborne, Intermediate '71: you asked him to stand off and he nearly did, but then he could not see where he was going to land, so he put in a short stride. Because you were already leaning up his neck he hit it hard and you fell off.

Hold him together, with your legs on him and sit tight and still.

Aintree Fence, Wylye '71: you didn't want to gallop at it, because if he threw a big jump you would probably peck on the 6 ft 6 ins drop. So you turned him into it going at a good but not head-long pace; it felt just right. Three strides out you knew you were coming in wrong, so you sat still. When he realised it was a drop he steadied right up, and taking off very close to it he almost rocked on top, landed vertically, pecked badly and very nearly turned over. You should have counteracted his steadying by urging him forward but you would have had to start five or more strides out, then if you knew he was coming in wrong you could have continued to urge him, but

not asked him to stand off. But it never occurred to you he'd alter his pace and you were only concerned with not going too fast. Next time *ride* him BALANCED into it.

Seat over drops: for a really firm seat, don't just think of keeping your weight back and body upright. Try and imagine there is a fence a couple of strides after the drop, which means you've got to gather him up both ends as he lands. In this way you will be really gripping over the drop, e.g. Ski-jump and Quarry at Badminton '72.

Ski-jump, Cirencester '72: the angle of the take-off ramp was too steep, making the horse's hindlegs slip as he took off and creating a very unseating jump which you weren't expecting. Watch for this and always inspect take-offs."

Corners

"ATTACK these at an increasing pace; when once you have your line, *ride* it. DIVIDE the angle, and be straight on that imaginary line.

NB Windsor: the corner fence was cleverly sited with crowd ropes in such a position that you had to go right out and almost touch them before turning into the fence. This is becoming a popular trap. As at Windsor, when there is another fence beyond the corner, you must give him as long a line as possible to look at both elements, otherwise he will become muddled.

When jumping corners, find a mark far away on the other side of the fence

and don't take your eyes off it for a second. Same applies to any fence you don't like.

BE STRAIGHT for a corner further away than for a normal fence. The horse *needs* more time to adjust."

Coffins

"Badminton '73: you dropped the contact before the fence and hit him; he was going too fast with his head in the air and therefore couldn't see where he was aiming. NO martingale on. Beware now: he will remember the very uncomfortable passage through that fence next time.

Remember his refusal at Osberton '73 when he was looking around him at the running crowd instead of concentrating on the coffin ahead. You must get his attention in front of an obstacle. If necessary stop him and start again, well back from the fence, just to say, 'Come here. Listen.'"

Ins and Outs

"Four yards is very short for Be Fair on flat ground; five yards is barely enough and you must hitch him back in front of these fences.

The coffin at Punchestown was nearly six yards, and the ditch six feet wide; he did this with no stride. However, at Wylye '71 (Open Championships) he put half a stride in between the sleeper bank and post and rails, only three yards apart, and hit it very hard. This was because you turned in too sharp; you only had one straight stride and possibly weren't quite collected enough, consequently less impulsion. He didn't have time to make his arrangements, and so he jumped very short up the bank and had to scramble to get out over the rails. You must be firmer and collect up more when you have to turn in sharp to a fence.

At the Silage Pit, Tidworth '71, you were prepared for him to jump the trakehner badly before the bank and rails. However, he jumped the trakehner beautifully, and you were so surprised you sat there. As it always will, the upright sleeper bank slowed him up, and he got half a stride in on the bank and hit the rail hard. Be ready for anything and always have plenty of controlled impulsion into a bank and rail.

Crookham '73 – Be Fair popped through a combination measuring five yards and seven and a half yards. Having slowed right up and changed into third gear, he bounced the first distance and put a stride in the second.

Normandy Bank, Badminton '72 and '73 –. In 1973, remembering the too fast and flat '72 effort, you went too slowly. He hadn't enough impulsion to throw a big jump and had to put in a stride on top – hair-raising."

Memos

"Man anticipates all but that which befalls him. Expect the unexpected."

"If at the last minute you realise you are in a very tricky situation, leave it to the horse and SIT STILL with EYES UP. Don't throw your hands and weight forward, thereby unbalancing him – just *sit still* and keep legs on."

"The smallest or most innocuous-looking fence will cause the most trouble. When you find such a fence say, 'What's difficult?' not 'That's easy.'"

"You'll never win unless you finish the course, faultlessly. You must not let your concentration go when the worst is over. You must NOT let yourself be relieved – keep apprehensive – *you've relaxed once too often.*"

"'Despair is destruction.' If you make a mistake, take a pride in keeping cool. If you despair and say, 'It's all over,' you'll make another mistake. GET ON WITH IT; you owe your horse the rest of the round.

NB Badminton'72 – you made two bad mistakes after your run-out at Tom Smith's Walls."

Approach Guide

1	2	3	4	5	6	LR 1	LR 2
Coffin – Bounce in Sunken Road – Bounce in	Coffin – Stride in Sunken Road – Stride in Quarry-Drop Single/Double Bounce (Distance: 12'+) Turning Combination Into Water – Deep & No Drop Bank & Rail Combination	Simple Upright Wall Double Combination Corner		Triple Bar Open or Water Ditch Ditch Towards or Away Rail Across Open Water Trakehner	Unfinished Bridge Hedge Steeplechase Fence	Steps Down Ski-Jump	In Water Very High Irish Bank
		Upright & Drop Single/Double Bounce (Distance: 15'+) Under Roof Hay Rack Into Water – Drop	Rail & Ditch Spread & Drop Bullfinch Into Water – Shallow				
	Bounce & Drop into Water						
	Fence at Base of Sharp Slope Drop followed by Bounce	Bank (Small) – Irish or Sleepered	Normandy Bank Parallel				
		Elevated Landing					
		Steps up Table – No Ground Line Drop Fence into Combination Fences in Shadow	Table – Filled in				
	Rails followed by Drop into Water						

This chart is maybe of some help if only to portray how wide is the range of different 'approach gears' to cross-country fences.

I have used gears 1 to 6 and low ratio gears 1 and 2 (slow trot and less slow trot) to help decide the type of speed of approach and the amount of revs that are necessary.

He was hard and tough and wiry – just the sort that won't say die –
  There was courage in his quick impatient tread;
And he bore the badge of gameness in his bright and fiery eye,
  And the proud and lofty carriage of his head.

From *A Man from Snowy River*
by Banjo Patterson, 1895

Thank you.